My First at Day Care

Janelle McGuinness

Jes VP

For Nina and Jessica.

Thank you to my family and friends for the support and encouragement, Damien, Tina and Giannina.

Published by MCG Ventures Pty Ltd
BOX 23 / 9 Rohini Street
Turramurra NSW 2074
Australia

For more information about the author visit:
www.jmcgbooks.com

Cover design and illustrations by Jes VP

ISBN: 978-0-9953822-9-9

My First Day at Day Care

 Can you find me throughout the book?

Today, is my first day at day care.

I wonder what it'll be like?

Mom says it will be lots of fun.

Will I get to ride a big bike?

I walk through the large front gate
and kids are everywhere just like me.
There are toys and balls all around,
as far as the eye can see.

Mom walks with me to my classroom.

Behind her legs I hide, not to be seen.

I see books, tables, dough and puzzles.

Wow, everything looks bright and clean!

"Hello, my name is Kate.
I'm your carer today.
Welcome to the Blue Room!
It's time to start to play."

"First, we say hi and learn what day it is.
Then we'll look at some books and read aloud.
Soon, we are going to paint with glitter.
We know this really draws a happy crowd."

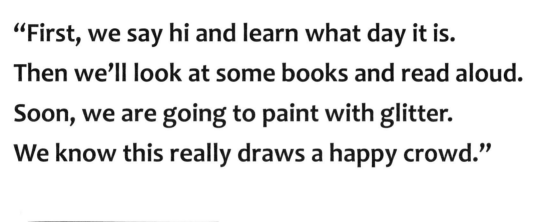

It's time for Mom to say goodbye.

Does she really have to go?

She says "see you soon" and hugs me.

Will she come back? I really hope so.

Kate sees I am a little bit sad.

She gives me a hug and lots of care.

"Do not worry, Mom will be back soon.

Come in and put your bag over there".

I walk over to a boy named Tom.

He is building a tower with blocks.

I ask quietly, "can I play too?"

He says, "sure, grab some more from the box."

We all line up straight to go outside.

There are many things for me to try.

Which activity should I do first?

Off I run, not a time to be shy.

I jump around, skip, and throw a ball.
Climb on the monkey bars and play games.
Drive tractors in the sandpit with Tom
and play monsters with long funny names.

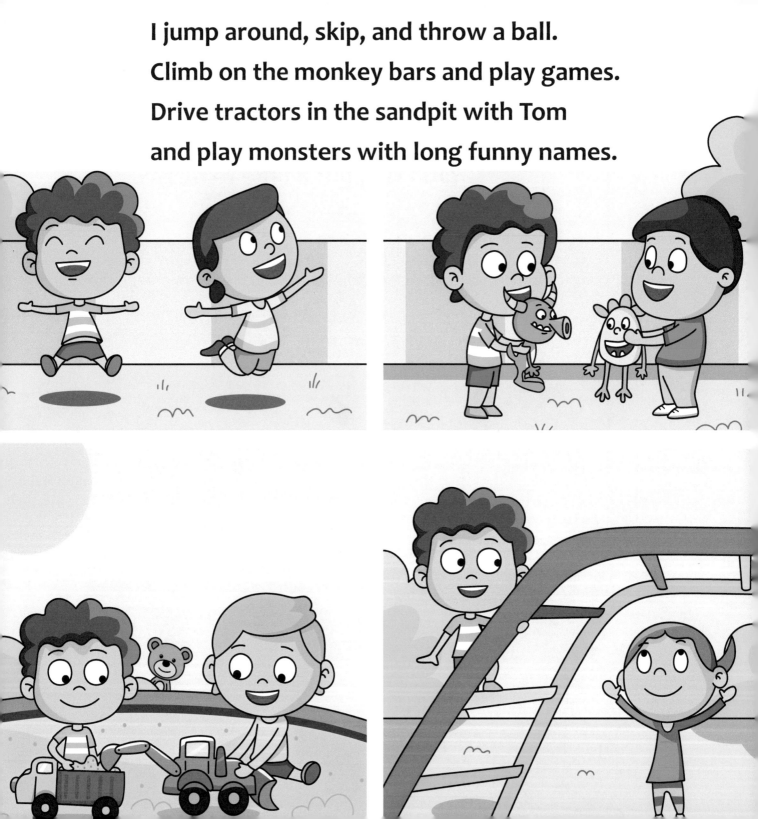

After playing, it's time for our lunch.
We all wait patiently for our food.
With perfect manners, we eat our meal,
staying until the last bite is chewed.

After lunch, it's time for a nap.
We get our little beds ready.
It's like having a sleepover.
I go and grab my soft teddy.

When we wake, it's dancing time.
We all hold hands and dance around.
All my favorite tunes are playing.
Music, it's such a glorious sound.

Somebody taps me on the shoulder.

It's my Mom! She asks, "Are you ready?"

She has come from work to pick me up.

Is it really that time already?

"How was your day my dear?
Did you have lots of fun?"
"Yes, there was lots to do.
And tears? There was not one."

Thank you for purchasing this book!

I hope your young reader enjoyed it as much as I enjoyed writing it. If you liked the book, I'd be really appreciative if you could spare a couple of minutes to write an online review. Reviews for indie authors, like myself, mean so much.

Want a free coloring book?

If you'd like to download a *free* coloring book with pictures from this book, **sign up at** **http://www.jmcgbooks.com/freebies.html**

Visit www.jmcgbooks.com for more information.

Interested in my other books?

Come Out Mr Poo!

Ready or Not, Here I Come!

My First Day at Daycare

Secret School Spy Squad series:

Mission 1 – Lost Lunchboxes

Mission 2 – Germs Galore

Mission 3 – Shrinking Students

Mission 4 – Hair-raising Hair

Mission 5 – Zapping Zombies

Coming Soon:

Princess? Not Me!

What was Cool When Dad was at School

Made in United States
Troutdale, OR
01/02/2025